BLUE MOOSE

Weekly Reader Children's Book Club presents

BLUE MOOSE

Written and illustrated by MANUS PINKWATER

DODD, MEAD & COMPANY, New York

Library of Congress Cataloging in Publication Data

Pinkwater, Manus.
    Blue moose.

    SUMMARY: A man who runs a restaurant on the
edge of the big north woods meets a talking blue
moose that moves in and spends the winter serving as
head waiter.
    [1. Moose—Fiction.   2. Restaurants, lunch
rooms, etc.—Fiction]   I. Title.
PZ7.P6335Bl   [E]   75-12575
ISBN 0-396-07151-1

Weekly Reader Children's Book Club Edition

for Otsu

The moose shines bright,
The stars give a light,
And you may kiss a porcupine
At ten o'clock at night.

CONTENTS

The moose is blue,
Your wish will come true.

MOOSE MEETING

MR. BRETON had a little restaurant on the edge of the big woods. There was nothing north of Mr. Breton's house except nothing, with trees in between. When winter came, the north wind blew through the trees and froze everything solid. Then it would snow. Mr. Breton didn't like it.

Mr. Breton was a very good cook. Every day, people from the town came to his restaurant. They ate gallons of his special clam chowder. They ate plates of his special beef stew. They ate fish stew and Mr. Breton's special homemade bread. The people from the town never talked much and they never said anything about his cooking.

"Did you like your clam chowder?" Mr. Breton would ask.

"Yup," the people from the town would say.

Mr. Breton wished they would say, "Delicious!" or, "Good chowder, Breton!" All they ever said was, "Yup." In winter they came on skis and snowshoes.

Every morning Mr. Breton went out behind his house to get firewood. He wore three sweaters, a scarf, galoshes, a woolen hat, a big checkered coat, and mittens. He still felt cold. Sometimes animals came out of the woods to watch Mr. Breton. Raccoons and rabbits came. The cold didn't bother them. It bothered Mr. Breton even more when they watched him.

One morning there was a moose in Mr. Breton's yard. It was a blue moose. When Mr. Breton went out his back door, the moose was there, looking at him. After a while, Mr. Breton went back in, closed the door, and made a pot of coffee while he waited for the moose to go away. It didn't go away; it just stood in Mr. Breton's yard, looking at his back door. Mr. Breton drank a cup of coffee. The moose stood in the yard. Mr. Breton opened the door again. "Shoo! Go away!" he said.

12

"Do you mind if I come in and get warm?" the moose said. "I'm just about frozen." The moose brushed past him and walked into the kitchen. His antlers almost touched the ceiling.

The moose sat down on the floor next to Mr. Breton's stove. He closed his eyes and sat leaning toward the stove for a long time. Mr. Breton stood in the kitchen, looking at the moose. The moose didn't move. Wisps of steam began to rise from his blue fur. After a long time the moose sighed. It sounded like a foghorn.

"Can I get you a cup of coffee?" Mr. Breton asked the moose. "Or some clam chowder?"

"Clam chowder," said the moose.

Mr. Breton filled a bowl with creamy clam chowder and set it on the floor. The moose dipped his big nose into the bowl and snuffled up the chowder. He made a sort of slurping, whistling noise.

"Sir," the moose said, "this is wonderful clam chowder."

Mr. Breton blushed a very deep red. "Do you really mean that?"

"Sir," the moose said, "I have eaten some very good

chowder in my time, and yours is the very best."

"Oh my," said Mr. Breton, blushing even redder. "Oh my. Would you like some more?"

"Yes, with crackers," said the moose.

The moose ate seventeen bowls of chowder with crackers. Then he had twelve pieces of hot gingerbread and forty-eight cups of coffee. While the moose slurped and whistled, Mr. Breton sat in a chair. Every now and then he said to himself, "Oh my. The best he's ever eaten. Oh my."

Later, when some people from the town came to Mr. Breton's house, the moose met them at the door. "How many in your party, please?" the moose asked. "I have a table for you; please follow me."

The people from the town were surprised to see the moose. They felt like running away, but they were too surprised. The moose led them to a table, brought them menus, looked at each person, snorted, and clumped into the kitchen.

"There are some people outside; I'll take care of them," he told Mr. Breton.

The people were whispering to one another about the moose, when he clumped back to the table.

16

"Are you ready to order?"

"Yup," the people from the town said. They waited for the moose to ask them if they would like some chowder, the way Mr. Breton always did. But the moose just stared at them as though they were very foolish. The people felt uncomfortable. "We'll have the clam chowder."

"Chaudière de Clam; very good," the moose said. "Do you desire crackers or homemade bread?"

"We will have crackers," said the people from the town.

"I suggest you have the bread; it is hot," said the moose.

"We will have bread," said the people from the town.

"And for dessert," said the moose, "will you have fresh gingerbread or Apple Jacquette?"

"What do you recommend?" asked the people from the town.

"After the Chaudière de Clam, the gingerbread is best."

"Thank you," said the people from the town.

"It is my pleasure to serve you," said the moose. The moose brought bowls of chowder balanced on his antlers.

18

At the end of the meal, the moose clumped to the table. "Has everything been to your satisfaction?" he asked.

"Yup," said the people from the town, their mouths full of gingerbread.

"I beg your pardon?" said the moose. "What did you say?"

"It was very good," said the people from the town. "It was the best we've ever eaten."

"I will tell the chef," said the moose.

The moose clumped into the kitchen and told Mr. Breton that the people from the town had said that the food was the best they had ever eaten. Mr. Breton rushed out of the kitchen and out of the house. The people from the town were sitting on the porch, putting on their snowshoes.

"Did you tell the moose that my clam chowder was the best you've ever eaten?" Mr. Breton asked.

"Yup," said the people from the town, "we said that. We think that you are the best cook in the world; we have always thought so."

"Always?" asked Mr. Breton.

"Of course," the people from the town said. "Why do you think we walk seven miles on snowshoes just to eat here?"

The people from the town walked away on their snowshoes. Mr. Breton sat on the edge of the porch and thought it over. When the moose came out to see why Mr. Breton was sitting outside without his coat on, Mr. Breton said, "Do you know, those people think I am the best cook in the whole world?"

"Of course they do," the moose said. "Do you want me to go into town to get some crackers? We seem to have run out."

"Yes," said Mr. Breton, "and get some asparagus too. I'm going to cook something special tomorrow."

"By the way," said the moose, "aren't you cold out here?"

"No, I'm not the least bit cold," Mr. Breton said. "This is turning out to be a very mild winter."

GAME WARDEN

THERE WAS a lot of talk in town about the moose at Mr. Breton's restaurant. Some people who had never been there before went to the restaurant just to see the moose. There was an article in the newspaper about the moose, and how he talked to the customers, and brought them their bowls of clam chowder, and helped Mr. Breton in the kitchen.

Some people from other towns drove a long way with chains on their tires to Mr. Breton's restaurant, just to see the moose. Mr. Breton was always very busy waiting on tables at lunchtime and suppertime.

The moose was always very polite to the people, but

23

he made them feel a little uncomfortable too. He looked at people with only one eye at a time, and he was better than most of them at pronouncing French words. He knew what kind of wine to drink with clam chowder, and he knew which kind of wine to drink with the special beef stew. Some of the people in the town bragged that the moose was a friend of theirs, and always gave them a table right away. When they came to the restaurant they would pat the moose on the back, and say, "Hello, Moose, you remember me, don't you?"

"There will be a slight delay until a table is ready," the moose would say, and snort, and shake himself.

Mr. Breton was very happy in the kitchen. There were pots of all sorts of good things steaming on the stove and smelling good, and bread baking in the oven from morning to night. Mr. Breton loved to cook good things for lots of people, the more the better. He had never been so busy and happy in his life.

One morning, Mr. Bobowicz, the game warden, came to the restaurant. "Mr. Breton, are you aware of Section 5—Subheading 6—Paragraph 3 of the state fish and game laws?" said Mr. Bobowicz.

"No, I am not aware of Section 5—Subheading 6—Paragraph 3," Mr. Breton said. "What is it all about?"

"No person shall keep a moose as a pet, tie up a moose, keep a moose in a pen or barn, or parlor or bedroom, or any such enclosure," said Mr. Bobowicz. "In short, it is against the law to have a tame moose."

"Oh my," said Mr. Breton, "I don't want to do anything against the law. But I don't keep the moose. He just came along one day, and has stayed ever since. He helps me run my restaurant."

Mr. Bobowicz rubbed his chin. "And where is the aforesaid moose?"

Mr. Breton had given the moose one of the rooms upstairs, in which there was a particularly large bed. The moose just fit in the bed, if he folded up his feet. He liked it very much; he said he never had a bed of his own. The moose slept on the bed under six blankets, and during the day he would go upstairs sometimes, and stretch out on the bed and sigh with pleasure.

When Mr. Bobowicz came to see Mr. Breton, the moose had been downstairs to help Mr. Breton eat a giant breakfast, and then he had wandered back to his room to enjoy lying on his bed until the lunchtime customers arrived. He heard Mr. Breton and Mr. Bobowicz talking. The moose bugled. He had never bugled in Mr. Breton's house before. Bugling is a noise that no animal except a moose can really do right. Elk can bugle, and elephants can bugle, and some kinds of geese and swans can bugle, but it is nothing like moose bugling. When the moose bugled, the whole house jumped and rattled, dishes clinked together in the cupboard, pots and pans clanged together, icicles fell off the house.

"I AM NOT A TAME MOOSE!" the moose shouted from where he was lying on his bed.

Mr. Bobowicz looked at Mr. Breton with very wide eyes. "Was that the moose?"

The moose had gotten out of bed, and was clumping down the stairs. "You're flipping right, that was the moose," he growled.

The moose clumped right up to Mr. Bobowicz, and looked at him with one red eye. The moose's nose was touching Mr. Bobowicz's nose. They just stood there, looking at each other, for a long time. The moose was breathing loudly, and his eye seemed to be a glowing

28

coal. Mr. Bobowicz's knees were shaking. Then the moose spoke very slowly. "You . . . are . . . a . . . tame . . . game warden."

The moose turned, and clumped back up the stairs. Mr. Breton and Mr. Bobowicz heard him sigh and heard the springs crash and groan as he flopped onto the big bed.

"Mr. Bobowicz, the moose is not tame," Mr. Breton said. "He is a wild moose, and he lives here of his own free will; he is the headwaiter." Mr. Breton spoke very quietly, because Mr. Bobowicz had not moved since the moose had come downstairs. His eyes were still open very wide, and his knees were still shaking. Mr. Breton took Mr. Bobowicz by the hand, and led him into the kitchen and poured him a cup of coffee.

DAVE

NOT VERY FAR from Mr. Breton's house, in a secret place in the woods, lived a hermit named Dave. Everybody knew that Dave was out there, but nobody ever saw him. Mr. Bobowicz, the game warden, had seen what might have been Dave a couple of times; or it might have been a shadow. Sometimes, late at night, Mr. Breton would hear the wind whistling strangely, and think of Dave.

The moose brought Dave home with him one night. They were old friends. Dave was dressed in rabbit skins, stitched together. His feet were wrapped in tree bark and moose-moss. An owl sat on his head.

"Dave is very shy," the moose said. "He would ap-

preciate it if you didn't say anything to him until he knows you better, maybe in ten or fifteen years. He knows about your gingerbread, and he would like to try it." While the moose spoke, Dave blushed very red, and tried to cover his face with the owl, which fluttered and squawked.

Mr. Breton put dishes with gingerbread and applesauce and fresh whipped cream in front of Dave, the moose, and the owl. There was no noise but the moose slurping, and Dave's spoon scraping. Mr. Breton turned to get the coffeepot. When he looked back at the table, Dave and the owl were gone.

"Dave says thank you," the moose said.

The next night Dave was back, and this time he had a whistle made out of a turkey bone in his hat. After the gingerbread, Dave played on the whistle, like the wind making strange sounds, the moose hummed, and Mr. Breton clicked two spoons, while the owl hopped up and down on the kitchen table, far into the night.

HUMS OF A MOOSE

ONE DAY, after the moose had been staying with Mr. Breton for a fairly long time, there was an especially heavy snowfall. The snow got to be as high as the house, and there was no way for people to come from the town.

Mr. Breton got a big fire going in the stove, and kept adding pieces of wood until the stove was glowing red. The house was warm, and filled with the smell of applesauce, which Mr. Breton was cooking in big pots on the stove. Mr. Breton was peeling apples and the moose was sitting on the floor, lapping every now and then at a big chowder bowl full of coffee on the kitchen table.

The moose didn't say anything. Mr. Breton didn't say anything. Now and then the moose would take a deep breath with his nose in the air, sniffing in the smell of apples and cinnamon and raisins cooking. Then he would sigh. The sighs got louder and longer.

The moose began to hum—softly, then louder. The humming made the table shake, and Mr. Breton felt the humming in his fingers each time he picked up an apple. The humming mixed with the apple and cinnamon smell and melted the frost on the windows, and the room filled with sunlight. Mr. Breton smelled flowers.

Then he could see them. The kitchen floor had turned into a meadow with new grass, dandelions, periwinkles, and daisies.

The moose hummed. Mr. Breton smelled melting snow. He heard ice cracking. He felt the ground shake under the hoofs of moose returning from the low, wet places. Rabbits bounded through the fields. Bears, thin after the winter's sleep, came out of hiding. Birds sang.

The people in the town could not remember such an unseasonable thaw. The weather got warm all of a sudden,

and the ice and snow melted for four days before winter set in again. When they went to Mr. Breton's restaurant, they discovered that he had made a wonderful stew with lots of carrots that reminded them of meadows in springtime.

MOOSE MOVING

WHEN SPRING finally came, the moose became moody. He spent a lot of time staring out the back door. Flocks of geese flew overhead, returning to lakes in the North, and the moose always stirred when he heard their honking.

"Chef," the moose said one morning, "I will be going tomorrow. I wonder if you would pack some gingerbread for me to take along."

Mr. Breton baked a special batch of gingerbread, and packed it in parcels tied with string, so the moose could hang them from his antlers. When the moose came down-

43

stairs, Mr. Breton was sitting in the kitchen drinking coffee. The parcels of gingerbread were on the kitchen table.

"Do you want a bowl of coffee before you go?" Mr. Breton asked.

"Thank you," said the moose.

"I shall certainly miss you," Mr. Breton said.

"Thank you," said the moose.

"You are the best friend I have," said Mr. Breton.

"Thank you," said the moose.

"Do you suppose you'll ever come back?" Mr. Breton asked.

"Not before Thursday or Friday," said the moose. "It would be impolite to visit my uncle for less than a week."

The moose hooked his antlers into the loops of string on the packages of gingerbread. "My uncle will like this." He stood up and turned to the door.

"Wait!" Mr. Breton shouted. "Do you mean that you are not leaving forever? I thought you were lonely for the life of a wild moose. I thought you wanted to go back to the wild, free places."

"Chef, do you have any idea of how cold it gets in the

wild, free places?" the moose said. "And the food! Terrible!"

"Have a nice time at your uncle's," said Mr. Breton.

"I'll send you a postcard," said the moose.

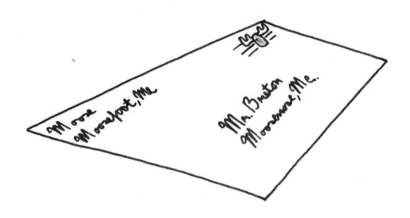